belle MEDIA

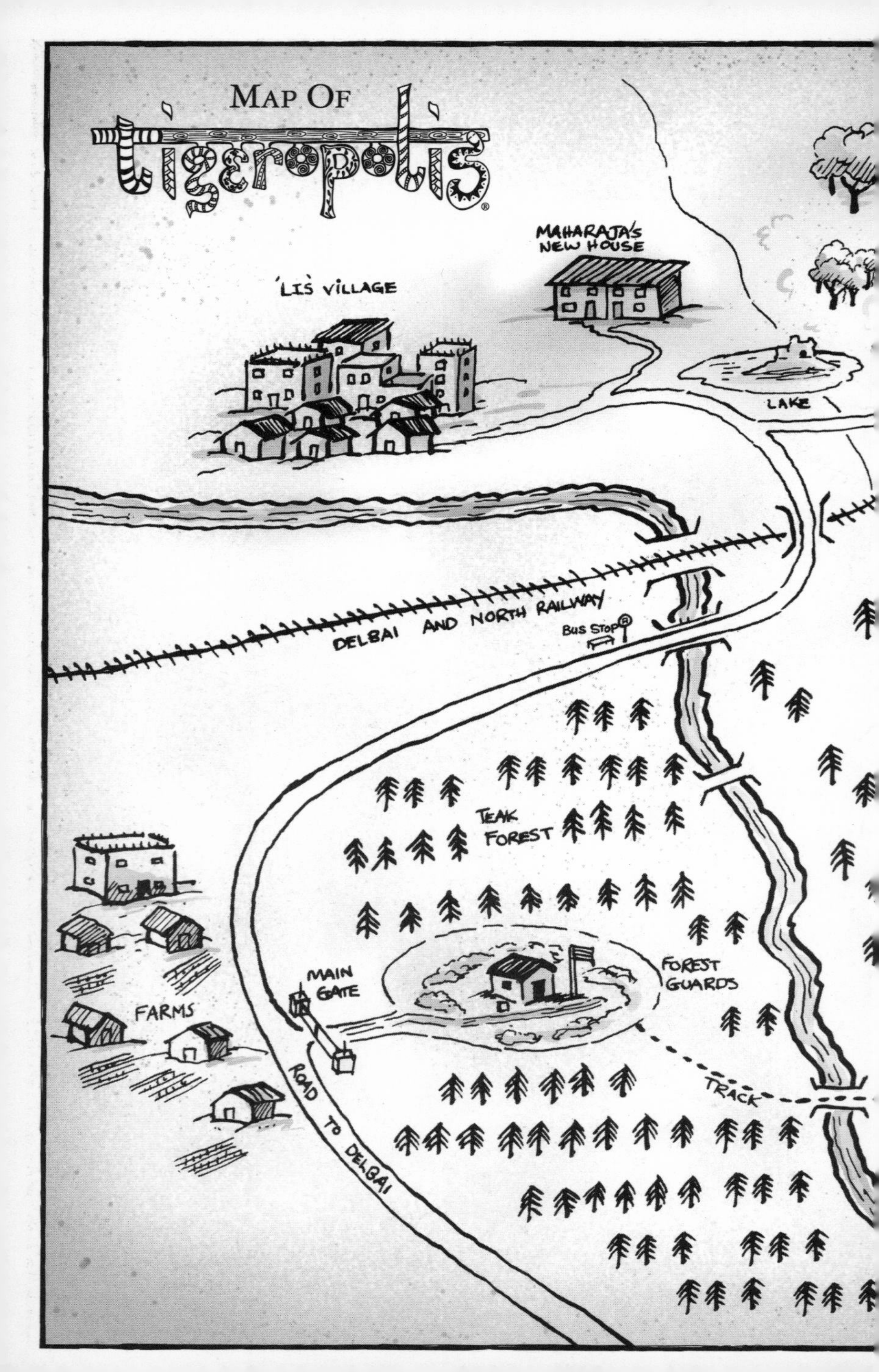
Map Of
tigeropolis®
MAHARAJA'S NEW HOUSE
'LI'S VILLAGE
LAKE
DELBAI AND NORTH RAILWAY
BUS STOP
TEAK FOREST
MAIN GATE
FOREST GUARDS
FARMS
TRACK
ROAD TO DELBAI

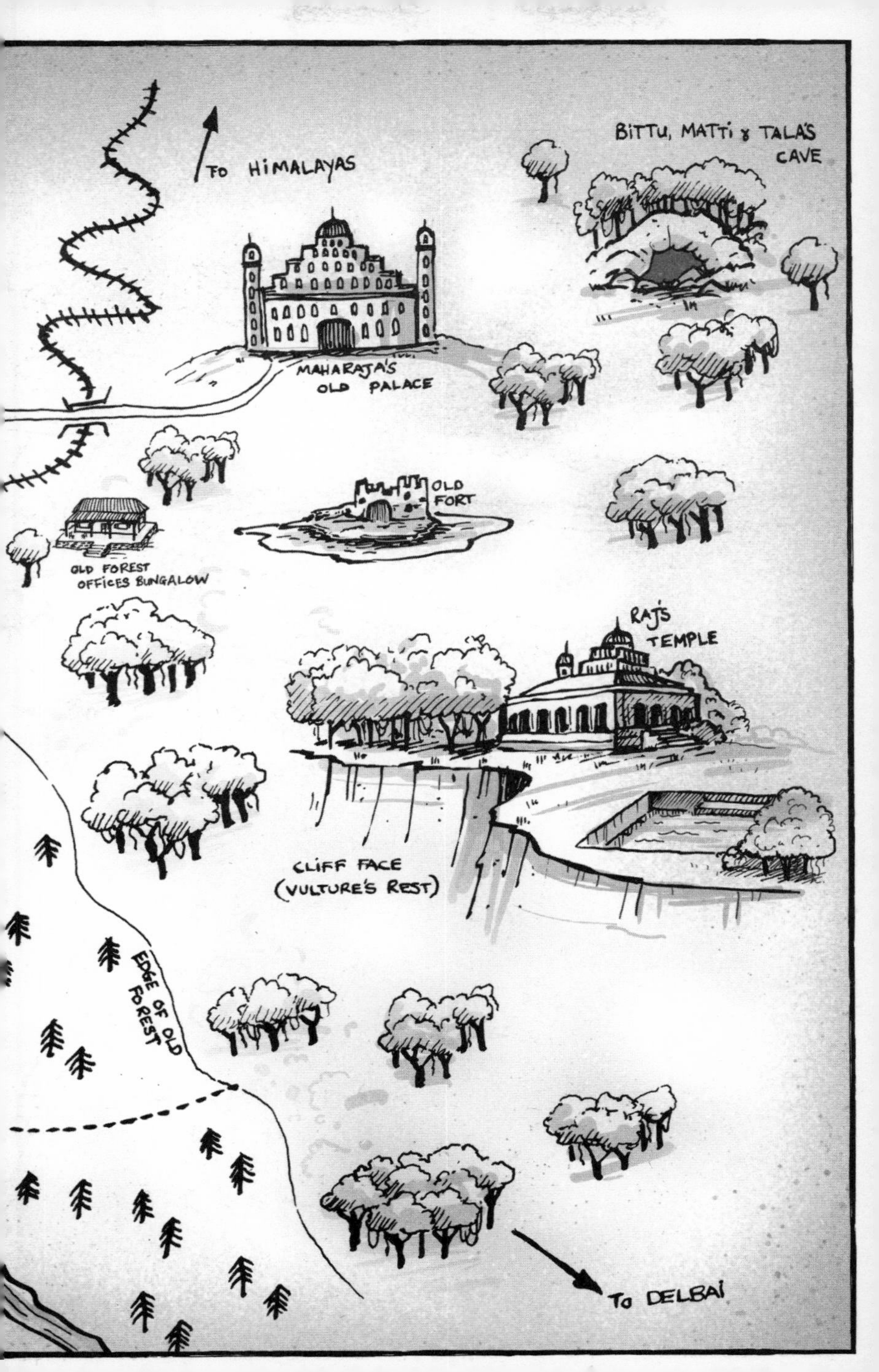
TO HIMALAYAS
BITTU, MATTI & TALA'S CAVE
MAHARAJA'S OLD PALACE
OLD FORT
OLD FOREST OFFICES BUNGALOW
RAJ'S TEMPLE
CLIFF FACE (VULTURE'S REST)
EDGE OF OLD FOREST
TO DELBAI

The Tigeropolis Series

BEYOND THE DEEP FOREST

THE GRAND OPENING

CAUGHT IN THE TRAP

Book 1

Beyond the Deep Forest

By R. D. Dikstra

First Published in Great Britain in 2015 by Belle Media Ltd

Tigeropolis: a Belle Media Book

ISBN Number 978-0-9927462-1-6

Illustrations by Matt Rowe
Designed by Andrew Cook, **essense** design
Tigeropolis title design by Grace Anderson
Printed in the UK

Published by Belle Media Ltd, London
36 Ferry Quays, 5 Ferry Lane, London, TW8 0AT

Tel +44(0) 208 568 3556
www.bellemedia.co.uk

This book is dedicated to all the Forest Guards,
Rangers, Policemen, Conservation Experts, Scientists,
and Volunteers who have dedicated their lives to
protecting India's rich and diverse wildlife,
and in particular its magnificent *Tigers*.

Chapter 1 – The Discovery

Bittu was tired… and just a little lost.

He'd been having a great time chasing a little sambar deer through the jungle. They had run past the old abandoned fort, past the tumbled-down whitewashed

stone temple, past the old hollowed-out water storage pond filled with the darkest greeny-black water you could imagine, and down a twisty, sandy track to the very edge of the old sal forest where he lived.

He knew he should have stopped. But chasing sambar was such fun and he felt sure just a little while more and he would have caught him. Twenty minutes later, however, he realized the sambar must have given him the slip and disappeared through a hole in the fence somewhere back at the little crossroads.

'Oh well… next time,' thought Bittu.

So where was he now? He had never been beyond the deep forest on his own and he began to realise the teak plantation that he was now moving through was totally different from anything he had ever seen before. Regimented rows of straight, tall teak trees; all spaced out equally, almost identical in height, each tree looking exactly the same. It felt odd, a bit unnatural, and almost completely devoid of life.

Many years earlier, the trees had been planted to provide a ready supply of wooden sleepers for the Delbai &

North Western Railway. Of course, by the time the trees were fully grown, things had moved on, needs had changed and now they used concrete sleepers instead. So the trees were just left to keep on growing higher and higher, and with every year that passed, they made this part of the forest darker and darker.

No matter which way he looked, everything looked exactly the same and to make matters worse the forest floor was covered in the largest, crackliest leaves Bittu had ever seen. Indeed the forest floor was buried in so many leaves that it was even difficult to see where he had come from. There was not even a single animal in sight to ask the way and he was clearly lost.

Suddenly, and just before he started to really panic, in the distance, through a small gap in the trees, he realized he could just about make out a small white-washed hut.

He decided this was his best hope of finding the way home. Nonetheless he was wary of meeting any humans that he might find there. He started towards the hut, moving slowly, worried the crackly leaves might give him away. After a few tense minutes he entered a small clearing. Luckily it was covered in soft grass that was quiet enough to walk on and just about tall enough to provide him with some cover. The chowki hut was roughly square and made of whitewashed mud bricks, with a corrugated iron roof.

Directly facing him was an open door and there were small sash windows on either side of the hut, both open to provide a through draught and let in some cool air on a hot April day.

He came right up to the side of the building and, rising up on his rear paws, he could almost peek in through the open window. Inside was an office, it had a beaten earth floor and was sparsely furnished: just a single dark wooden desk, two chairs, one on each side where the two guards, dressed in their standard issue khaki uniforms, sat talking. In one corner stood an old grey metal 4-drawer filing cabinet, and beside it a little wickerwork side table with a slightly battered electric kettle, two mugs, a few tins and bottles all neatly grouped together on one side. The dark wooden desk was almost entirely covered with bundles of official-looking, yellowing papers, all tied up with little red ribbons in the old-fashioned way that some lawyers firms still do.

In one corner, Bittu could see an old, black bakelite phone with a silver dial and, pinned up on the wall, at the far side of the room was a large faded hand-traced map. Written in bold felt tip pen right across the top was the heading *Tigeropolis Tiger Sightings Last 5 Years.*

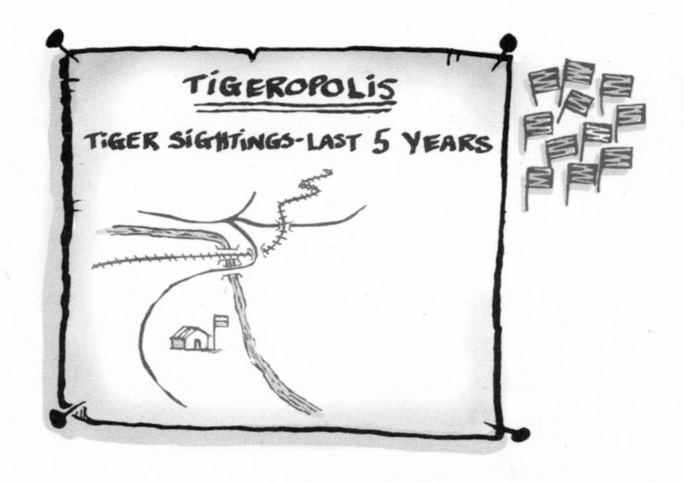

To the right of the map was a chaotic collection of little black-and-amber striped flags, all set up and ready to record any tiger sightings. But on the map itself there were none.

The older, grey-haired man was looking worried and kept looking down at an official-looking piece of paper he held in his right hand. He shook his head.

'What's to become of us? Just what is to become of us? I don't believe this can be happening', he said scrutinizing the document. 'They want to close Tigeropolis!'

Akash, the younger, more junior but definitely the more tubby of the two, put down the large piece of chocolate cake he was just about to bite into. 'Perhaps someone actually looked at one of the monthly reports we've been sending in to HQ, and finally noticed that we have never, ever sighted a tiger here in Tigeropolis, well not for twenty years. Look at the sightings map, Mr Mistry – not one!' he said pointing to the map on the wall.

He went on, 'And we're supposed to be a tiger sanctuary! But there are no tigers and we have nothing to guard… absolutely nothing!

'Even Delbai must find that hard to justify'. He stopped

for a brief moment, distracted by the cake and its delicious smell of chocolate, and then continued, 'and we have no local support from anyone in the town. With no tigers to see, no-one ever eats at the restaurant or stays at Mr Singh's hotel, and when was the last time anyone paid Mr Patel to go on a jeep ride through the park? I can't remember a time'.

'Yes, yes', interrupted Mr Mistry, 'but I bet it's Mrs Banerjee that's behind closing Tigeropolis. She has always wanted to have the forest cut down so that the Ministry could build a shiny new road straight through to Delbai – that way she could drive there and back again in time for tea'.

'That's progress I'm afraid,' Akash sighed, finally stuffing the cake into his mouth.

'Can't they see the forest is important?' said Mr Mistry. 'If the forest was gone, Tigeropolis closed, where would the birds, the langurs and the sambar live? How would children learn to appreciate nature and enjoy the trees?… And what about us? How would we earn a living Akash? You have a wife and family to support.'

Akash gulped another mouthful, 'HQ doesn't care… it's simple… no tigers, no tourists, no future.'

Still outside eavesdropping, Bittu had heard enough. It was late and he urgently needed to find his way home. Over in the far corner of the little clearing, much to his relief he could just make out the outline of a narrow track. The sun was starting to get quite low, and he needed to be back before dark.

Chapter 2 – Owning Up

That night Bittu sat with his mother and older sister Matti beside the fire in their snug little cave, deep in the deepest part of the wood. They lived there, just the three of them. They moved in just before his father's accident. In all honesty, Bittu couldn't remember a great deal about his father. Big and powerful, with a wonderful toothy grin... he was fast. Very fast. He had been 100-metre inter-park champion two years running.

Apparently, one day while he was out hunting for vulture eggs for their tea, the path broke away from the cliff. It was a narrow, difficult path that ran up to the ruined lookout post on Vulture's Rest. Bittu knew the spot well. His father must have fallen over 200 feet that day and was killed outright. It was dangerous being a tiger living in the wild, even without any humans about.

It happened when Bittu was still very small. It always made him shudder when he went past the spot and it was rather sad to think about it all and to realise his father wouldn't be there to play with him or see him grow up. But it also made him determined to live up to his father's memory, and to be the tiger his father would have wanted him to be. Bittu wanted to make his father proud.

As he sat there by the fire, he thought 'what would Dad want me to do at a time like this?' He knew he would get into trouble for leaving the old sal forest as he'd been told countless times not to go too far. But despite the possibility of getting into trouble, he thought he ought to tell his mother what he'd heard, and that the forest guards were worried about Tigeropolis.

'Mum?' he said rather sheepishly.

'Yes, lambkin', she replied distractedly as she darned a hole in a pair of Bittu's football socks, in readiness for the big game on Saturday.

'You know how we're not supposed to go beyond the old forest..?'

'Indeed', she said sternly, suddenly taking an interest.

'Well… what if… what if a *friend* of mine… accidently… went beyond the old forest into the teak plantation and… accidently of course… what if that *friend* heard something very important? Should he tell anyone? Even if it might get him into trouble?'

'Oh, surely that would never happen with anyone you knew Bittu darling? You are such a good boy… and I know you, or rather your *friend*, would never do that… would they?'

'But supposing it did happen,' said Bittu, 'what then?'

'Well, then I think your friend would be very wise to tell his mother exactly what had happened… and as soon as possible,' she added firmly, now looking directly at him.

Bittu took a big deep breath and started to tell the story. Matti put down her colouring pen and waited to hear what her naughty little brother had been up to, hoping he would finally get a telling off. Tala listened intently and tried to keep calm when she heard how far Bittu had gone and how close he had come to an encounter with the Forest Guards.

Realizing the seriousness of the situation and the threat to their life in the Park, Tala told them both not to worry and that tomorrow they would all go off to consult with old Uncle Raj.

'Wise old Uncle Raj will know what to do,' Tala said, 'he always does.' Relieved he had unburdened himself, Bittu soon fell into a deep sleep after such an eventful day.

Next morning, just as the sun came up and before it got too hot, all three set out for the old temple. Uncle Raj lived right on the edge of the cliff at the far side of the ruined temple that Bittu had run past so excitedly the previous day.

Bittu and Matti liked going there even although it took them over an hour to reach the temple. There were always interesting things to do: passageways to explore, old ruins to play in, and crumbling statues to clamber over. Bittu's favourite was a giant 3 metre-high stone tortoise, somehow still balancing a great big marble ball on its nose. Matti liked the statue of a reclining Buddha that was almost completely buried in a thicket of giant grass. There were lots of little hidey-holes at its base that she could sneak into and spring out of at any moment to pounce on her little brother when he was least expecting it.

As usual, they found Uncle Raj lying fully stretched out, relaxing and enjoying the morning sun at a favourite place by the steps of the temple courtyard.

The temple had been built by Buddhist monks but it had eventually been abandoned as they were unable to provide a year-round supply of drinking water. They had dug out a huge stone-lined pond to try to gather the monsoon rains but it was never enough. Now it provided the perfect place for Raj to contemplate the world as he watched the wading birds, monkeys and other wildlife drinking and playing together in the glistening waters.

'Hello Uncle Raj,' said Tala, as Raj lazily opened one

eye to see who was approaching, 'Well hello Tala,' Raj said, pausing to take a huge yawn. 'What brings you all here on such a fine morning?'

'Well Raj, it seems little Bittu was chasing sambar again and, as usual, did not know when to stop. I just don't know how many times I've told him not to go beyond the forest and into the teak plantation, but will he listen?' she said looking sternly in Bittu's direction.

'Anyway,' she said calming down, 'it seems he ended up at the old Chowki hut that the forest guards still use in the clearing next to the river. You know, the one with the flag? Well, Bittu overheard them say they're planning to close Tigeropolis, knock it all down and build a new shopping centre and goodness knows what else instead!'

Bittu interrupted excitedly, 'and all because their boss Mr HQ has decided there are no tigers left in the park. None in twenty years they said.'

'No tigers, *that they have seen*, you mean,' corrected Uncle Raj gruffly.

'True,' said Tala, 'but this is serious. What will we do? This is our home, Raj.'

Bittu and Matti looked at their mother slightly nervously. Her voice sounded much more worried than they'd heard before.

'And it's not just the park closing,' she continued, 'it's the road. With the road comes more people, with more people comes more demand for farmland. More farmland means even more trees get cut down and before we know it, there's no forest left. Not one stick. Look at what happened to Mumbett Park. It'll be red blobs everywhere, painted on every tree. A tree gets a red blob and down it comes. And if all that happens, where do we go to live undisturbed and in peace?

'Oh, Raj. What can we do?' she said anxiously.

'Most worrying I agree,' said Raj, pulling himself up slowly to standing, stretching out his slightly stiff old limbs. 'Hmmm, let me think.'

'How soon did they say it would close Bittu?'

'I'm not sure, but I think at the end of the season,' replied Bittu.

Raj looked concerned and contemplated, pacing around as he did so.

'Most worrying indeed,' he muttered quietly to himself.

Bittu was thinking too and suddenly sat up.

'But... but *we're* tigers. *We* live here!' he exclaimed.

'Why can't we just run up to the forest guards and tell them its all okay, that there's been a terrible mistake, that we're tigers and we can all stay. Once Mr HQ hears this, surely Tigeropolis can stay open?'

'The boy's right,' exclaimed Tala, and smiled proudly at the cleverness of her young son.

'Not so fast' said Raj. 'It's years since any of us had anything to do with forest guards or any people for that matter.' The others fell silent as he went on…

'Don't you remember why we kept ourselves to ourselves for so long? Before Grampa's incident, it all seemed harmless fun: the tourists, the celebrity status, the visits from the film crews, the royalty, polite requests for photographs, the odd selfie, even supplying inky paw prints for children's autograph books. But after a while it all became too much. It wasn't just Grampa's injury that disturbed us, the people just wouldn't let us alone. They were coming from hundreds of miles around, and began to expect more and more of us tigers.

'Eventually it wasn't enough for them just to know that tigers were living here, they wanted personal souvenirs, hair clippings from our best winter coats, our old milk teeth and they'd even scoop up our old dried tiger droppings! Someone once even tried to pluck out one of my whiskers as a souvenir – very painful and undignified. Mind you, they didn't try that again, I can tell you.

'And on top of that,' he continued, 'they had expectations that were totally unrealistic – they expected us to behave exactly like the tigers they had all seen on TV. Action: morning, noon and night. No-one seemed to appreciate that real life just isn't like the movies. It didn't occur to them that these TV programmes were all scripted and filmed over many months, that the producers only picked the exciting bits from hours and hours of footage and then edited them all down into a half hour 'show.'

They wanted life in Tigeropolis to be '*as seen on TV*' he said flicking his claws in the air indicating imaginary quotation marks.

'They didn't want tigers like us – civilized hard-working tigers, tigers that stayed home at night, looked after their cubs and relaxed in the evening sun with their G&Ts. They didn't want to hear about us reading newspapers, checking emails and doing the crosswords. No, they wanted tigers that roared all day long, tigers that went around fighting, chasing and hunting other animals. Blood and action, that's what they wanted – dangerous wild tigers.'

'**MAN-EATERS!**' cried Bittu excitedly.

'No Bittu, not man-eaters. Just tigers that scared people a bit' said Raj. 'But even so, I'm afraid what they wanted was just not us. And that's the reason we left.'

'Oh dear,' said Tala, 'you're right, Raj. I remember now, you're bringing it all back. How very awkward. But perhaps the tourists have moved on in the last twenty years? Perhaps today's humans would treat us better?'

'Perhaps. But we don't really know how to behave in the way they now want,' said Raj.

'Can't we learn?' said Bittu interrupting. 'It sounds fun, all that roaring and chasing. I think they said that the park will close in a month. Surely we can learn to roar and hunt in a month? It can't be that difficult.' And after saying that, he gave out a funny little choking sound in a first rather pitiful attempt at a roar:

'Rrruarrrr, rrr, cuhughh, cuhughh'.

'Possibly, possibly,' muttered Raj, ignoring Bittu's feeble attempts. Raj strode purposefully across towards the old banyan tree that shaded the ruined temple courtyard and disappeared inside its veil of roots and branches. He ferreted about for a few minutes in the special pink suitcase he'd found abandoned by the roadside.

'It won't be easy… it's all so long ago.'

'Ah yes, here we are… my old *Scouting for Tigers* handbook. Those were the days…' he mused to himself while dusting off the cover with the back of his giant furry paw.

'What fun your Uncle VJ and I had back then,' he sighed thinking of his youth, 'giving the old Maharaja the slip as he tried to track us down. He was riding way up on the top of his massive, lumbering hunting elephant, crashing and banging his way through the forest in hot pursuit. Luckily, the Maharaja was very short sighted so he needed to be quite close to us to actually take a shot.' Raj chuckled to himself. 'We were too fast and too clever for him. He was also quite rotund and not very keen on going too fast over rough terrain in case he fell off, so he could never keep up with us.'

Matti suddenly became much more interested in the conversation. 'Hunting on elephants, what fun!'

...She was in a dream, imagining herself on her own elephant, dressed in a beautiful sky-blue sari, diamond earrings jangling and dangling in the breeze as she sat perched on a golden howdah. A servant boy in a turban sat cross-legged beside her, cooling her with a giant white ostrich-feather fan and helped shade her from the heavy heat of the midday sun.

Billowing coloured silks hung from the howdah's canopy, occasionally fluttering as a gust of wind caught the finely woven material. All the while, her trusted mahout, dressed in scarlet tunic, encouraged his elephant on into the jungle in search of the mythical white unicorns of Lis...

'It was indeed great fun,' said Raj rather tersely, bringing her back from her daydream with a start. Matti quickly composed herself, realizing she'd been a little carried away.

Raj continued, 'but it was dangerous too – remember your Uncle and I were on foot. It was the Maharaja that was on elephant back, and he was trying to shoot us.

Thankfully, after about an hour or so, the Maharaja always ended up calling a halt to the chase. He was a man of habit and four o'clock was tiffin time.

'You could set your watch by it. No matter how close he might be to catching us, or what else he might be doing, at 4pm he stopped. He would then slowly and carefully dismount, very much in a huff with his mahout, who would once again be blamed for failing to catch us. He would then slink off, defeated, down to the river where his servants were setting up his afternoon tea by some shady spot. Your Uncle VJ and I would then creep back through the undergrowth to take a look.

'We used to play a game to see how close we could get without being spotted. Creeping up through the undergrowth we'd watch as he sat back on a huge pile of deep-blue monogrammed silk cushions scoffing his scones, cream and jam and drinking his favourite blend of Earl Grey tea. He had it specially shipped in from Four-Tum's in London, don't you know.

'We were usually never more than three metres away in the bushes… How we kept from laughing out loud at the sight of him, I just don't know, especially as he usually ended up with a great big dollop of cream right on his nose, having been just a little too greedy with his helpings.

'Now, where was I?' Uncle Raj muttered, getting back down to business. 'Oh yes, the book. Yes, he said flicking carefully through the pages, 'this book might prove very handy. Very handy indeed…'

'Right, all back here tomorrow morning bright and early everyone… we have important work to do.'

Chapter 3 – Lesson One

'Roll call!' announced Raj in his most serious voice, as the group shuffled into place and stood more or less to attention.

'Tala?'

'Here!'

'Bittu?'

'Here!'

'Matti?'

...Silence.

'Matti?'

...Silence.

'Matti...? ...Bittu where is that sister of yours?'
'Matti...?
'*Ma-tti...?*'

'Coming Uncle!' said Matti, a little embarrassed at being seen to be late. She stepped out from behind a large curious-looking decorative cherry wood box sitting on the ground at the edge of the clearing and ran to join the others.

'Good at last, all present and correct,' Raj said, ticking off the final name and putting down his clipboard.

'So. …**Good morning tigers!**' he shouted out in his best 'parade-ground' growl.

They responded half-heartedly, and at different times, so that all anyone could make out was a mixed-up mumbled, 'orning', 'ning', 'ncle Raj', or sounds to that effect.

'Louder please, and let's have it all together, I want some enthusiasm here,' he barked, a little annoyed at their lack of application to what was actually the easiest task of the day.

'Again. Lets try again… **Goooood Morning Tigers,**' he shouted.

'Good Morning, Uncle Raj,' they all shouted back, but still a little out of synch.

'That's the spirit… great… well done in the ranks,' he said proudly, glad of even the semblance of some improvement. It was going to be a long day, he thought.

He paced up and down, then turned to the group and announced rather sternly, 'Today we begin *Operation Jungle Growl*. An operation vital to the survival of Tigeropolis, so pay close attention to everything I say.'

There was a pause…'*Operation Jungle Growl*? What's the old boy on about?' murmured Tala to herself. 'Oooh, dear, I think he's finally lost it.'

'Don't you think Uncle Raj is taking this all a bit too seriously, Mum?' whispered Matti, a bit concerned at where this was all going.

'Yes,' Tala responded to the cubs, 'I think he thinks he's back in the army.'

'And that was years ago,' she added. 'I wouldn't mind, but for all his talk, he was only the Regimental Mascot. He might have a medal for it, but it was all parades and durbars as far as I can understand. The nearest he got to any fighting was when he was MC at the inter-services boxing.'

As she spoke, she had to suppress a chuckle at the thought of a young Raj, tail swishing, whiskers carefully waxed and proudly leading a parade of the 52nd Indian Frontier Rifles, complete with gold regimental sash across his chest and a pipe-band marching along behind.

'Quiet in the ranks!' roared Raj.

'Lets begin…

'And I see Matti has already discovered that we'll be deploying the latest teaching technology to enhance our training regime,' he said walking towards the cherry wood box that Matti had been playing with earlier.

'What? That?' exclaimed Tala in genuine disbelief.

Bittu and Matti looked across at the strange contraption. They'd never seen anything like it before and were excited to discover what it was. It had a folding lid, a long bent handle stuck out on one side and emerging from the back was what looked like an ancient traffic cone, only upside down.

'Grandad's old wind-up phonograph – surely not,' said Tala.

'Oh, is *that* what it is?' said Matti, 'I thought it was some sort of experimental hair dryer for elephants,' she giggled.

'It's a loud speaker,' corrected Raj, 'in fact, to be absolutely accurate, it's a Mark II Tigerette. Never bettered I believe, indeed I have it on some authority that Queen Victoria herself had one. Gold plated of course, but

Outside, an old battered jeep was parked beside a tall thin flag-pole from which fluttered a slightly frayed Indian flag. Over the doorway a little half-forgotten notice board announced:

Welcome
Keep Out - Strictly No Visitors
By Order of Forest Dept

Inside he could just make out the voices of two forest guards. It seemed they were having a very serious conversation and certainly paid no attention to the little tiger outside.

This was the first time Bittu had been so close to real, live, people. Normally whenever they saw anyone in the forest, he and his sister Matti did what their mother always told them to do; they were to run off, hide under a bush, keep very quiet and wait for the humans to go. But Bittu was curious. Many years earlier the tigers in Tigeropolis had retreated back into the deeper forest because of an 'incident' and, from that day on, they had kept well away from all humans.

All Bittu knew was that the 'incident' was something to

do with tourists. A jeep full of tourists had knocked his grandfather from his bicycle as he cycled back from drawing fresh water at the river. According to his mother, the jeep had come far too fast round a blind bend, and on the wrong side of the road, and then… WHAM! His grandfather had no chance of avoiding it. He was in plaster for weeks.

In those days, tourists were able to bring their own cars into the tiger parks and were allowed to drive more or less wherever, and whenever they wanted. Chaos. After the accident, the rules were changed. From then on, no private vehicles were allowed, people had to have official drivers, everyone had to follow designated routes and they could only go into the parks at set times of day – early morning and late afternoon. Welcome as the changes were, Bittu's family decided it was just too much trouble living near the humans. So, as soon as his grandfather was up and about, the family moved deep into the heart of the old forest, and effectively disappeared from sight.

But today Bittu was intrigued and he kept moving closer to find out what was going on.

otherwise identical. Would not be parted from it.

'And, I can tell you, if it's good enough for Her Majesty, it's more than good enough for you lot!'

'Raj, that was over 100 years ago,' said Tala.

'Well, that may be,' he said, somewhat crestfallen at the poor reaction his clever ideas were receiving, 'but it's the key to our success, so pay attention.'

He had been particularly pleased with himself the previous night, remembering he still had the phonograph and the set of 78rpm records. It was right at the back of the cupboard under the stairs leading up to his winter perch in the banyan tree. And now here they all were making fun of him.

'I'm not asking you to admire the tech. All I need is for you to listen,' he said rather curtly, while holding up a large black shiny shellac disc. 'Listen carefully, and you will hear what good old-fashioned tiger roaring actually sounds like… and then I want you to copy exactly what you hear.

'Get it right, and tourists will flock here,' he added as he began to wind up the record player with his tail. He then placed the disc on the spinning turntable and carefully set the needle down on track 1, side 1 of *Sounds of the Jungle: 'Tiger's Roar at Dawn'*.

'Remember, repeat exactly what you hear,' said Raj at his sternest.

Matti, Bittu and Tala listened very carefully as the track began. *Crackle, pop, click, ROAR, hiss, click, ROAR, crackle, crackle!* went the Mark II Tigerette.

They took a deep breath, smirking, glanced at each other and carefully began to repeat… *"Crackle, pop, click, ROAR, hiss, click, ROAR, crackle, crackle!"* all in perfect unison (albeit stifling giggles).

'Not like that!' said Raj, now visibly angry and not at all appreciating the joke.

'Do it again!'

'Roar' they repeated, a bit half-heartedly.

'Better…' said Raj. 'At least you're all trying. Once more, but louder please. And with feeling!'

'Roar!' they went again.

Raj was getting impatient.

'No! What we're aiming for is **'ROARRRRR!'** and he opened his mouth the widest Bittu and Matti had ever seen it. Wide enough to see all of his great big white shiny teeth, and right down the back of his throat – in fact nearly wide enough to see the roti he'd had for breakfast.

'ROAR!' they tried again, but still rather weakly.

'You are supposed,' said Raj, 'to be fearsome kings of the jungle. Not a bunch of meditating pilgrims bound by an oath of silence! …So, deep breaths everyone… Hold it …Now imagine you're blowing out all the candles on your birthday cake... but from right across the other side of the room!

'So, on the count of three. One and two and…'

'ROARRRRR!' they went in unison, soooo loudly that everything else in the jungle suddenly fell silent.

'ROARRRRR!' they repeated, beginning to enjoy themselves.

'ROARRRRR!' 'ROARRRRR!'
'ROARRRRR!' 'ROARRRRR!'

'I think you've got it! Yes, by Jove you've got it… you've really got it!' said Raj excitedly.

'ROARRRRRRRRRR!'

they went again triumphantly.

'Lesson 1: Tick. Excellent. I think we can say *'mission accomplished'*, said Uncle Raj happily. Things, it seemed, were finally looking up.

'Lesson Two. Stalking. Now, what does it say here, he mused, thumbing through his copy of *'Scouting for Tigers'*, until he stopped at the correct page, adjusted his glasses and read out carefully…

> *'Tigers stalk their prey by positioning themselves down wind of their target to avoid their scent being detected.*
>
> *Then, slowly, silently and purposefully they creep up to within striking distance of their target. In doing so they use any available natural cover. Long grass is particularly helpful for avoiding detection, but care needs to be taken not to disturb the vegetation too much, as unusual movement of long grasses or any associated rustling noises might alert nearby animals.*
>
> *Monkeys can be particularly problematic to tigers as they spend much of their time high up in trees observing activity in the forest. They often spot tigers on the prowl and can disrupt a tiger's hunting routine.*

It is therefore recommended that tigers avoid working in areas with excessive monkey populations.'

'Seems quite simple, I'm sure you'll agree,' he said putting down the book.

'Right let's have a go. Matti, see any monkeys around?' he asked.

'No, Uncle,' she replied, 'I think all the monkeys are off on a field trip to the fort today – it's Monkey Monday.'

'Good no problems there then. Bittu, now see if you can sneak up on that young sambar over there,' he said pointing at a cute little deer that had just wandered out of the woods and into the clearing and was now enthusiastically tucking in to some particularly lush grass at the side of the waterhole.

Bittu did as he was asked and set off. He moved slowly towards the little sambar who was still munching away happily. Bittu did not have any natural cover to hide his approach (unlike the example given in the book), so instead, Bittu improvised. He tried to look as innocent as possible, consciously looking in every direction, except in the direction of the sambar. At one point he even started whistling a little tune to himself, in an attempt to appear disinterested and nonchalant, possibly just out for a stroll, and certainly not a threat to any little sambar that might happen to be nearby. And all the while, of course, and ever so slowly and purposefully, he was closing the distance between himself and his target.

Then, just as he got within about 3 metres… disaster: the sambar looked up…

'Hello Bittu, what are you doing here?' she said.

'Oh... hi Bindi,' Bittu said awkwardly, '…yes, nice morning,' he said, his voice tailing off as he tried to think of something more to say.

Bindi continued, 'Did you hear that awful noise a few minutes ago? I was just walking through the woods, and it gave me quite a fright, I can tell you. It was a sort of roaring sound, really weird.

'The park authorities should do something about it. Must have been some yobs. Disgraceful. The neighbourhood's really gone to the jackals.'

'Yes, yobs...' muttered Bittu, nodding and just a wee bit embarrassed. He thought about owning up, but decided it was easier to keep quiet and avoid having to explain.

Raj called out from across the meadow 'Bittu, stop chatting and come back, we've work to do. Good try… but perhaps the whistling is best left out for now.'

Bittu blushed a little as he mumbled something to Bindi about how he had to go off somewhere with his family, and ran off back to the group, relieved not to be facing any more awkward questions.

'Matti, your turn,' said Raj. 'What about seeing what you can do with that peacock over there by the pool? Do you think you could sneak up behind him quietly and surprise him? He seems to be rather busy preening his tail feathers, so hopefully you can do a better job than your little brother.'

Matti crept forward on her tiptoes.

Tippy-toe, tippy-toe, tippy-toe… she moved silently across the rough ground, stopping every few metres just to steady herself and to check she hadn't been spotted. Finally, she was directly behind the peacock, who was busy admiring his reflection.

'BOO!' she shouted at the top of her voice, while also clapping her paws hard together with a great THWAACK to add to the effect. The peacock jumped half a metre into the air with fright and gave out an almighty AWWWWWKKK, AWWWWKKK. He flew off in a great flurry of flapping feathers and squawks. The scene delighted her little brother. Yes, thought Bittu, finally his sister had put all those ballet lessons to good use. Result.

'Great. Well done both of you… maybe a little more practice required for you Bittu, but we're getting there. What might be a good idea now is a little 'field trip' to see how it's done by the professionals. Tomorrow we'll go over and visit Cousin Vinni in Ranthgarh – he has made it one of the top tourist sites in the country and it's definitely worth a look.

'They have lots of tourists there every day, so he can tell us much more.'

Chapter 4 – Outward Bound

Next morning, bright and early, Bittu, Matti, Tala and Raj all set off for the bus stop outside the park. The stop was just after the bridge, about two miles from the Tigeropolis main gate, and not far from a small farming village.

It was years since any of them had been on the main road, but it was just as Raj remembered it. Nothing much had changed. In his younger days, he would often slip out of the park to watch the comings-and-goings. He enjoyed watching as people set out early each day piling onto the local bus with their baskets of fresh fruit and vegetables ready to sell in the markets in Lis and the surrounding towns.

He would watch, unseen, in the shadows of one of the many mango trees that lined the road. The mango trees had been planted a hundred and fifty years earlier by the Maharaja's grandfather, Mirza. He had planted the trees as a way of providing fresh fruit for travelling pilgrims. Each May thousands of pilgrims, thronged the road on their way to visit the old temple and would help themselves to the fruit as they trudged along the hot dusty track.

Today, however, there was no-one else at the bus stop – it was Tuesday and the market in Lis was closed. They all sat down on the little wooden bench beside the bus stop and waited.

Some time later, Raj said 'That's the third bus in a row

that's just driven right past. I don't understand. I'm sorry I even suggested getting the bus. I thought it would be a real treat since none of us have done it before, but none of the buses have even slowed down.'

'And not even an attempt at stopping,' added Bittu.

'If anything, the drivers seem to speed up when they see us!' exclaimed Matti, 'What can be the matter?'

'The buses don't even look full,' Tala grumbled… 'but I guess there must be a reason.'

'Look', said Matti, 'I'm even putting out my paw just like it says over there', pointing to a somewhat crudely painted and very faded public information poster on a notice board across the street with a giant hand waving down a bus.

'You'd think they didn't like the look of us,' said Bittu.

'One of the drivers should at least stop and tell us what's

going on and when the next bus will turn up. Its so rude,' Tala said in exasperation.

A little while later, Raj sighed again, now quite miffed. His plan to give the cubs a treat riding the bus was not working out. 'Oh, well, no matter, perhaps we should just walk – we need to get there before the light starts to fade and you never know who's prowling about in the jungle at night so we'll just get on and take the old road.'

Truth be told, despite putting a brave face on it, he was actually very disappointed indeed – he had been quite looking forward to a trip on the bus himself.

'The old road's more direct,' he rallied, 'and at least we won't have to cope with all the exhaust fumes from the traffic.'

And so the four tigers set off to join the forest track that linked the two reserves. It was quite a steep climb. Years earlier, it had been much easier to move between the two parks but gradually, bit by bit, the surrounding forest had disappeared; a little piece here, a little corner there, as farms sprung up and claimed more of the land.

Fences and buildings began to pop up everywhere. The path had therefore been diverted many times and was now mainly on the rougher, infertile ground that nobody had much use for (at least so far…). Given the speed of destruction, Tala wondered whether the stretch of forest between the two reserves might, one day, disappear altogether. Without a corridor through the forest, how would they manage to visit Cousin Vinni, Visha, or the rest of the family? Clearly, the bus was not an option: as had been demonstrated today, it was completely unreliable.

It was a long slog to Ranthgarh. They arrived about an hour after official closing time. The light was beginning to fade, the gates were locked and the little guard hut and ticket office were in darkness, the staff all away home for the night.

They snuck in through an old hole in the fence. It was about two-hundred metres from the main gate and near the spot where the elephants stayed at night. As a young cub, Tala remembered watching elephants when she visited the park with her own mother Sapna. She used to love seeing their expressions of relief and pleasure when the heavy howdahs used to transport the tourists

Chapter 4 – Outward Bound

were unbuckled from their backs. The mahoots then gave them a good wash and scrub down.

There were three elephants there that night and Tala told the cubs they would have to be very quiet as they went past, as elephants have a sixth sense when it comes to tigers and know when they are around.

Luckily, it was now after 5pm and the elephants were far too busy chomping away on tasty branches to care much about anything else, least of all tigers. With the elephants distracted by dinner, Raj, Tala, Matti and Bittu were able to walk straight past the enclosure without a single elephant giving them so much as a second glance.

Even although they had turned up without any notice at all, Cousin Vinni was delighted to see them. When they arrived, Vinni was crouched down by the side of the road with a big wooden hand stamp in one paw, pressing it down at regular intervals into the soft sand. Each time he did this, he left the impression of a perfect tiger footprint.

'What a surprise! Raj, Tala… and even the cubs, Bittu, Matti!' he exclaimed. 'Why didn't you say you were coming, Visha and I would have met you at the gate.

'Mwah, Mwah, Mwah,' they air-kissed, (well, as much as it's possible with whiskers).

'How are things at Tigeropolis?' Vinni enquired, 'presumably this is not just a social visit – your coming here unannounced must mean something more serious?'

'Yes,' said Raj, 'I'm afraid it's more than a social call – Tigeropolis is threatened with closure.'

'Goodness, that's awful,' said Vinni.

'Is there anything we can do? Space is quite tight, but you could move in here if you had to.'

'That's kind Vinni, but let's hope it won't come to that,' said Raj, trying to look on the bright side. 'Since we retreated back into the deep forest, it seems the tourist trade in the park has collapsed and people just don't visit any more, and unless we come up with something pretty soon, Delbai has earmarked Tigeropolis for closure.'

'They're set on building a road through it,' added Tala.

'Terrible, so you're here to get us to sign a petition?' said Vinni.

'No', said Raj, 'we've decided to reappear… to reappear and save the park'.

'Wow! Really?… Fantastic,' said Vinni, truly amazed his cousin had decided on such a radical approach.

'Yes, so much to re-learn and to set up, and of course such a lot has changed since my day,' said Tala.

'So, Vinni, you see, that's why we've come to see you,'

said Raj. 'We need your help and guidance – you have a great set-up here and we want to learn from the master. We don't have a moment to lose – I reckon if we're to have any chance of saving Tigeropolis we need to get the Minister's attention before the end of the month'.

'Got it Raj,' I'd be delighted to help. 'Come down to the house and we'll talk it over.'

'Great, thanks,' said Raj… 'but before we go, one question, what on earth are you doing here? It looks fascinating.'

'I do this twice a day,' he explained, holding up the hand stamp. 'The tourist vehicles spray up so much dust that they quickly cover up our fresh paw prints. Tourists are always excited when they see their first 'pug' mark, so I believe it's our duty to make sure they see them at their best.'

'But why do it with the stamp?' asked Matti.

'Good question, Matti,' replied Vinni smiling at his niece, 'simple really, I don't want to get my feet all covered in sand. Really messes up the house, and I'm always being told to wipe my paws before I go inside. The sand just gets everywhere...'

'And anyway, look at this,' he said, holding up the underside of the hand stamp he was using, '...this is a size nine pug. The tourists absolutely love to see a nice big crisp paw print, the bigger the better... and I'm only a size six, so this is actually better than the real thing.

'It makes a deeper mark, too, which is great for photographs, especially when the sun's low in the late afternoon. It casts beautiful shadows and I've seen some great shots of my handywork in *'Goodbye'* magazine – I tell you, it makes it all worthwhile.'

'Interesting', said Raj as he scribbled down the details and noted a few measurements.

'Oh, and that's a nice touch,' said Tala, 'adult and cute little baby cub prints, side by side... we definitely need to remember that.'

Vinni beckoned them back to the house. 'Let's get you settled with a nice cup of tea and we can talk more.'

After a quick wash and brush up they all sat down

together and Vinni continued with his advice…

'Let me see… well, I'd say, off the top of my head, and from our experience here, there are three key things to be aware of when dealing with tourists.

'Firstly, tourists are looking for an authentic experience, and they really like to see things that remind them of wildlife programmes they have seen on TV back home. So, forget the dancing displays, or having to put Matti on a unicycle.'

Matti smiled and giggled at the thought.

'Second, tourists are only active for short periods during the day: early in the morning – say from sunrise until about 8.30am – and again in the late afternoon. I don't really know what they do in between. A lot of them are foreign, UK, France, America, that sort of thing… so perhaps that's how they live back home. Or it might be the heat. In any case, they're only active for short periods, so it's important you're poised and ready for them when they are out and about'.

Bittu interrupted 'What, no lie-in in the morning?!'

he exclaimed, 'And what about my football practice after school? I'm supposed to be there from 4pm sharp if I'm to stay in the team.'

'Quiet Bittu, you'll have the rest of the day,' said Raj firmly, 'Vinni, please continue'.

Vinni began again, '…and lastly, Raj, its important to remember that tourists have paid quite a bit of money for their trip. They've come a long way, often from a crowded, noisy city and they want their day in the jungle to be really special and unique, *'awesome'*. It's a proper adventure for them, they have to feel as if they have worked hard for the experience, that they have really achieved something, so, if it's to live up to their dreams, it mustn't seem too easy. They want to go back home with plenty of stories to impress their friends.

'So yes, they've come to see tigers, but don't give it to them on a plate, don't let them see you too early on – create some anticipation and build suspense into the experience.'

'Right I get it,' said Raj, scribbling furiously, 'It all needs to be part of the whole package.'

Vinni continued, 'Here at Ranthgarh we usually try to leave the tiger sighting until about the last 40 minutes of their game drive... much more dramatic that way. By then they are beginning to fear they might never see a tiger and their guide is fretting about not being tipped if his clients go away disappointed.

'It sounds easy, Raj, but trust me, to really make it work it needs some careful planning on your side. You can't do the same thing each day. You need variety. You need to get to know the likely routes the guides will take, and the best places to break cover. You need to think too about the light levels for their photographs. You've got to work with them. If you're in too much shade they can't get a clear photo. Too little shade on a bright day and they'll miss the subtlety and sheer beauty of our stripes and markings.

'And remember, for each location you pick you'll need a good escape route. It needs to be a quick route back into dense jungle, to ensure you're not followed – otherwise you won't get any peace for the rest of the day.

'Does that all make sense Raj?... Tala?'

'Very helpful,' said Raj as he finished noting down all the points Vinni had just made in his little notebook.

'Bittu, Matti,' interjected Tala, 'why don't you let Cousin Vinni hear you roar? They've been practicing since Raj's lesson yesterday morning,' she said turning to Vinni. 'Cousin Vinni can tell you how you're doing.'

Vinni smiled.

'Not here mind, cubs,' said Tala, 'or you might deafen us. Go outside and give it a go on the count of three.'

'Right, yes,' they both said excitedly and scampered out the door into the little yard outside.

'On the count of three,' said Matti to her little brother – 'One, two …

'ROARRRRRR!' went Bittu.

'ROARRRRRR!' they both went. 'And once more for luck'…

'ROARRRRRR!'

Suddenly, and before anyone could say anything more, from somewhere outside in the park came an answering, and extremely loud:

'TOOOWEEEEP!'

'TOOOWEEEEP!'

'TOOOWEEEEP!'

It was the elephants at the gate. They'd finished their tea and were more alert.

'Excellent!' exclaimed Vinni. 'Could not have said it better myself. Cubs, let me translate: the elephants have just marked your roars ten out of ten! No need to practice any more tonight, I think.' The cubs beamed proudly.

'Oh yes, a couple of other points before we sit down to dinner,' added Vinni, 'I'm sure the tourists would love to see the cubs play-fighting. Nothing too violent, just pushing and shoving, that sort of thing… Matti, Bittu, are you up for that?'

'Absolutely not!' said their mother firmly, '*I'm* certainly not happy with that. I've just stopped Bittu from forever rolling about in the dirt, it gives me far too much washing and ironing. He's finally started to act like the young man he's supposed to be so I'm not having him going back to rolling about on the ground again, the tourists will have to manage without.'

Bittu looked disappointed.

'But you need to be professionals now, Tala,' said Vinni. 'You have to put on a really good show if you're serious about this so you might have to get used to all that extra laundry. It's all in a good cause.'

'And not only that, Tala,' he continued, 'as well as play-fighting, tourists really love to see tigers scratching tree bark and all that territory scent-marking stuff.'

'Scent-marking?' questioned Matti, amused by the expression.

'Yes,' said Vinni, slightly embarrassed he'd raised the subject, 'you know, doing your 'business' outside to mark your territory.'

'You mean doing a pee pee against a tree?' Bittu cried out excitedly, suddenly taking a great deal of interest in the conversation.

'Never, certainly not' said his mother, appalled at the very thought of her cubs acting like that. 'There will be none of that. Not now that we have the inside loo. Wild we may be, but we have standards.'

'Awwwww' said Bittu, clearly disappointed.

'Perhaps leave that bit to the adults then,' said Vinni deciding he had said enough for the moment and ought to move on.

Visha, Cousin Vinni's wife joined them, and after a good deal of chat and laughter over drinks, and the inevitable comments about how the cubs had grown, they all sat down to the wonderful dinner Visha had prepared.

As always with Visha's cooking, there were plates piled high with her special pakora, not to mention her dal, her aloo puri and her 'All India' winning recipe for paneer masala. All accompanied by a basket of fresh rotis and parathas and even a small helping of rice for everyone.

After dinner, Vinni suddenly got up and with a mysterious look on his face announced he was 'just popping out for a minute.' He'd had an idea.

Chapter 4 – Outward Bound

Chapter 5 – Tourists

The next day they were woken early – in fact, so early that it was still dark outside. Vinni was already up and standing beside their beds ready to get going.

'Morning explorers! Rise and shine! No time for breakfast I'm afraid – we need to be quick, its just coming up to dawn and the Park will be opening in 45 minutes. We need to get there quickly if we are to beat the queues,' he said ushering them downstairs.

In the hallway he made each of them put on a large, oversized, splodgy-green camouflage coat buttoned right up to the neck. He also gave them each a large dark brown, wide-brimmed hat that, in Bittu's case, was so big it almost sat on his shoulders. Matti and Bittu both giggled as they tried to walk, tripping over their giant coats, and all the while wondering what Cousin Vinni had up his sleeve.

Vinni led them outside, still not explaining anything. There, sitting in the centre of the driveway, was a large, shiny new, open-topped, dark green jeep. Its engine was running and, every so often, it would give a little shudder. Across the side of the vehicle it said, '*Jungle Explorer*' in big orange and black tiger-stripe lettering.

A uniformed guide was sitting at the wheel, one arm casually leaning on the door-frame, his bare elbow sticking out of the open window. He peered round to take a look at the odd looking group.

'This is Vikram,' said Vinni, 'he's the best guide in Ranthgarh, and a very close friend. I've asked him to help you.

'Vikram's going to take you on your very own special tourist trip, so that you can experience things for yourself.

'However,' he added sternly, 'we need to keep your visit secret, as otherwise it might scare the other tourists. If word got out that there were live tigers riding about in the park, goodness knows what would happen.'

'And of course there's also the tricky issue of tickets,' added Visha, who by this time had also joined them. 'It's better you go in as tourists – take these,' she said proffering a *Family Fun Pass*.

Driver Vikram opened the passenger door and helped them all on board.

'Remember, keep your coats fastened up and hats pulled well down over your ears,' shouted Vinni.

'Why don't we also wear our sunglasses,' offered Matti, putting on her own very large pair of Tan Rays. 'No-one will ever recognize us with these on.'

'Great idea, Matti, that really completes your disguise,' said Vinni.

Their disguise was indeed perfect… as long as you ignored the fact that no-one else in all of India was wearing thick, oversized camouflage coats with wide-brimmed hats in the near forty-degree heat, nor worried too much about the various sets of long bristling whiskers sticking out on each side of the passenger's faces!

They were quite satisfied with themselves, now setteled in the jeep and very excited to be having their own special VIP game drive through Ranthgarh.

'Now remember! Hats pulled down, tails in, and cubs,

absolutely no roaring! Good luck and enjoy the tour,' Vinni called out. He waved them off as they drove in to the park.

'Good morning, my most very special honoured guests,' said Vikram turning to address them.

'Welcome to your first tour of Ranthgarh, I am Vikram, I was born in one of the local villages and have lived here all my life. This is the most wonderful park in all India. On behalf of the *All India Exotic Travel Company Limited*, offices in Delbai, London and Mumbai,

we hope you have a wonderful trip and enjoy the sights, sounds and smells of the natural world. Please note: tips to driver not included in tour price. All gratuities gratefully received. Thank you for listening.'

'One other thing, my most honoured guests – if I put my hand up like this,' he said holding his open palm up in the air, 'you need to keep very quiet and make no sudden movements. Okay Dokay?'

'Okay Dokay,' they all nodded in unison.

'Great. Now let's go!' said Vikram.

So off they set. After a few minutes Vikram turned to Tala. 'Vinni says you're from Tigeropolis and you've never been on a game drive like this before… can that be right?'

'Well, Raj and I have,' said Tala, 'but it's a completely new experience for the cubs and they're really excited about it, right kids?'

Vikram started smiling, 'well, they've come to the right place. And it's a good time of year to see the wildlife.

The vegetation has died back a bit, so it's not too dense. We should be in for some really good wildlife spotting and remember you need to stay alert - our motto is '*You Snooze, You Lose.*' And with that advice, Vikram turned his attention to the road ahead.

They drove down twisty, dusty tracks for about thirty minutes, listening to the birds sing the last bars of their dawn chorus and, of course, watching out keenly for wildlife. It was seven o'clock, but it was already getting quite hot and Tala was beginning to realize that the heavy coats, whilst undoubtedly a good disguise, might not be such a great idea. Suddenly they felt the jeep slow down and Vikram raised his hand, signalling to them to be quiet. He pointed ahead, but slightly to the right.

'Look, to your right,' he said in a low voice, almost a whisper.

'Imagine the face of a clock – straight ahead is twelve. So now look there, just off to the right where two o'clock would be on your watch.

'Now, can you see?' he urged, 'there, just beyond the jacaranda tree… it's definitely a pair of jeeps. Looks quite a young group inside too… possibly from Delbai. Six… seven… yes, eight tourists if I'm not mistaken.

'And, look, I think there's a mother and at least three of her young in the right hand jeep.'

'Wow, yes,' said Matti under her breath, 'amazing… look at them in their bright t-shirts! They're so colourful. This is cool, I'm soooooo glad we came out to see this.'

'So many, this late in the season. Is that normal?' enquired Raj earnestly, trying to show how much he knew about tourist behaviour (after all, he'd watched quite a few 'holiday' programmes over the years on daytime TV, ones that detailed the everyday exploits of humans on their annual migrations).

'Well actually Mr Raj, you're right, this is quite unusual,' said driver Vikram, 'you're really lucky to get so much group interaction in April.'

He cut the engine and allowed his vehicle to quietly coast a few metres more before it finally came to a stop, half hidden from the tourists behind a large grey rock.

'Everyone, be very still and quiet… we don't want to frighten them,' said Vikram, 'let them come to us.'

'I don't think they have spotted us,' said Matti, getting excited, 'with luck they'll drive right up to us and we can get a really good look.'

And sure enough, the two jeeps kept coming nearer and nearer. Bittu was desperate for a closer look, and what would be his first sighting of tourists in the wild.

'That's right,' he said to himself, urging them on,'keep coming little friends, don't be frightened, we just want a proper look.'

'Ohhh, they're so cute!' Matti exclaimed.

'Shhhhhhhhh,' went driver Vikram.

'Bother, if only I had brought my camera,' said Matti. But even as she said it, she also remembered last year's Elephant Polo match at Tigeropolis.

It had been a great day and the elephants looked splendid in their team colours, with the sun glinting on their highly polished tusks. Instinctively, she'd taken out her phone to take a picture, but Uncle Raj reached out and pressed her paws downwards. Instead he told her to look around and tell him what she saw. Everyone else was clicking away furiously, uploading images and cheep, cheeping away. No-one was really watching the game.

'Cameras,' Raj said, 'are absolutely wonderful things – but, sometimes, in magical moments like this they can actually get in the way of people experiencing life. People should sometimes forget about taking photographs and just enjoy the moment.'

'Yes,' she thought, coming back to the present, 'what great advice.' Today she finally understood what Raj had been saying. 'That's what I'll do, I won't get distracted taking photos, I'll just sit back and enjoy.' Her uncle was very wise.

'Got it,' exclaimed Raj, 'perfect shot!' He was clicking away time and time again. 'This new 300mm lens is just fantastic,' he said, 'I'm so glad I brought it. Oh, I can't believe it, look, look, they're feeding, they're definitely eating crisps – what a photograph, *Tigerlife Photographer of the Year*, here we come!'

Matti looked at her uncle in utter disbelief – and after all he had said.

'Cameras down, please… NOW!' snapped Vikram.

'Tourists don't like too much attention, they're shy and easily spooked.'

Raj did as he was told and, somewhat put out, slipped his camera away and sat down quietly in the back seat to sulk. They watched the three jeeps come by, the leading vehicle slowing considerably as it approached – clearly the

driver was keeping a wary eye on them as they drove past.

'Take a look at their clothes: the bright pinks, the yellows and such vivid blues – most definitely city people from Delbai,' said Vikram knowledgeably, 'country people's plumage tends to be much more subtle and predominantly greens and browns.'

When the lead vehicle was only a few metres away, Bittu suddenly noticed a group of langur monkeys high up in the trees opposite. He knew langurs well – they were always up to mischief and needed to be chased off immediately. If you didn't chase them away, before you knew it, they would be off with anything they could lay their sticky little fingers on. Bittu was particularly concerned about his sandwiches – they were wrapped up in tin foil and monkeys can't resist shiny objects.

Instinctively, Bittu found himself turning to face the monkeys head on and began growling menacingly.

'Grrrrrrrrrrr,' he grrrrrrred, 'GRRRRRRRR,' he grrrrrrred more loudly still, and finally he showed his sharp white teeth to show them he meant business, and also wound up the volume… **'GRRRRRRRR.'**

'Grrrrrrrrrrr,' went Matti too, suddenly joining in when she realized exactly what was bothering her little brother.

Next thing she felt a sharp poke it the ribs from mum. 'Shhhhhhhh, both of you! Remember what Vinni said… no roaring, or growling, you'll frighten the tourists. Remember too, we're not supposed to be here!' she hissed under her breath to Bittu.

'Sor-ry,' mouthed Bittu, settling back into his seat, and giving the lunch bag one more concerned look. He still felt the need to glance menacingly in the direction of the langurs every now and then, just to make sure they weren't up to any mischief.

'Sorry,' repeated Matti quietly, 'we were just worried about losing our sandwiches. Those monkeys are soooooooo sneaky.'

Luckily, as it turned out, the Delbai group were far too busy talking to each other and admiring a massive elephant poo that sat gently steaming right in the middle of the road: it must have weighed ten kilos at least. So fascinated were they, that they hadn't paid any attention

to the growling sounds coming from other jeep or indeed the strange little group sitting together in their oversized coats, big hats and sunglasses.

Relieved at their good fortune, the tigers drove off, leaving the monkeys confused. They'd heard the growling quite clearly, but were at a total loss to work out where it had come from. All they could see were tourists. As far as they could tell, there wasn't a tiger in sight!

'We got away with it – they didn't notice any growling,' said Vikram. 'Tourists are just a bit slow and confused. Sharp as tacks at home, yes, but here? Here, it's all alien, nothing is familiar so they need everything pointed out.'

'The other guide saw us without a shadow of a doubt. He knows me. He knows I must have a good reason for driving four tigers about in disguise first thing in the morning, so he just kept quiet. Sanjeev is a good man.

'In fact, instead of pointing us out, he deliberately distracted his group, by loudly telling them how you can make paper from elephant dung – the average elephant produces enough poo each day to make over a hundred sheets of writing paper, that sort of thing.

That got them all talking about writing on it and what it smelt like.'

'Ewwwwwww, Elephant dung paper! So that's what people mean when they talk about recycling,' shrieked Matti, both grimacing and laughing at the same time.

'Yes. Well, thank you for that mature contribution Matti', said Raj.

'Its true, cubs,' added Vikram, 'elephants eat almost anything from grasses to big tree branches, but they have very poor digestion which means their poo is still pretty fibrous when it emerges. In munching up all that grass and mashing it up with all the other stuff they eat, it's just as though they were doing the first phase of the paper manufacturing process themselves.'

'My real point though,' said Vikram, 'is that tourists love all these extra little details and curious nuggets of information. It's something to tell everyone when they get back home. Elephants go through 250kgs of food a day, that generates fifty kilos of poo, eventually giving you a hundred sheets of paper, that sort of thing. Matti, you'd be surprised just how popular elephant dung notepaper is as a tourist souvenir. It's a real source of fun for the tourists and it seems they can always think of someone back home they want to send some to!' ☺

'Interesting,' said Raj, making a mental note that a small 'gift shop' might not be a bad idea if they did succeed in getting Tigeropolis back on the tourist map.

They drove on for another hour, passing odd groups of sambar scattered here or there by the roadside and at one point they even saw a wonderful muster of twenty peacocks all preening themselves by the river, their iridescent tail feathers spectacular in the morning light.

On they drove along a track that ran up to a wooded ridge and then even futher on up to a wide plateau. The track was pitted and rutted and covered in tyre tracks. It wound its way up to a small, domed white temple perched on the very edge of the ridge, dazzling in the bright sun. They could just make out about a dozen vultures circling effortlessly in the clear, blue, sky as they used their massive wingspans to ride the thermals rising up from the now sun-baked rock face.

'Just like home,' said Tala, still very much enjoying the ride.

Finally, after another half hour on dusty roads, they arrived at a small lake surrounded by trees. They turned left at the fork in the road and continued across a golden yellow meadow. Two metre high grasses swayed gently in the light breeze. At the far side, just at the edge of the wood, they came across a group of six or seven vehicles, all stopped in a line, engines off.

Everyone in the vehicles was standing up, looking intently to their left. Some were pointing excitedly, some were talking to each other in whispers. But mostly they were taking photographs and the air was full of their unmistakable sounds – autofocus beep-beeps, whirring motorized zooms and shutter 'clicks'.

Bittu and Matti were desperate to see what was causing such a stir. There was a real air of excitement.

Vikram drove slowly up to the back of the last vehicle in the group and switched off his engine. Then they saw

CLICK!
WHIR!
SNAP!
CLICK!
CLICK!
SNAP!
WHIR!
CLICK!
SNAP!
CLICK!

something totally enthralling. There, only six metres from the lead vehicle, on top of a large old tree stump, they could clearly identify their very own Cousin Vinni lying fully stretched out, and seemingly oblivious to all the fuss around him.

They couldn't believe it. Everyone in the other vehicles was absolutely fascinated at what Vinni was doing. But, as far as the cubs could see, he was doing, well, next to nothing at all – maybe not completely nothing; he did once swish his tail around a bit and then he turned his head and twiddled his ears to shoo off a few pesky flies that were buzzing about - but apart from that, not much.

Finally, in what was evidently the pinnacle of his performance, he gave a great open-mouthed yawn, fully exposing his giant canines. And as he yawned, you could immediately hear all the cameras furiously clicking away once again. It was just like the paparazzi following some celebrity as they walked up the red carpet at a major Bollywood premiere.

Bittu was sure Vinni had winked at him, but kept quiet, watching the master at work.

Cousin Vinni soon got up and started walking slowly and very deliberately along the side of the road, closely followed by all seven jeeps.

Pad, pad, pad… Vinni went on for another hundred metres or so before finally stopping. He turned slowly to look back at the vehicles one last time, gave out a loud defiant roar and disappeared back into the undergrowth.

The tourists clapped excitedly and some actually hugged each other in delight at their luck in seeing a wild tiger so close. Two minutes later, the tourists, completely happy with their morning's work, sat back down and their vehicles drove off, leaving clouds of dust billowing behind them.

Vikram turned to his passengers grinning, 'What a performer!

'What an absolute star,' he added, 'he loves it.' He then turned to Raj and asked quietly, 'home?'

'Yes, home,' said Raj, 'I think we've seen what we need to, thanks.'

Chapter 5 – Tourists

Chapter 6 – Debrief

'So that's it really,' said Vinni, putting down his cup of masala chai – he always had a cup of tea about eleven each morning. Savouring its rich milky flavour, he continued, 'it's the anticipation that's the key to people enjoying their day. Keep them waiting. We usually have them drive around for about two hours before we let them have a glimpse of us.

'Let them enjoy the park views first, get used to the heat and the dust, the noise and smells of the jungle. For most of them, it will all be an entirely new experience. They need time to take it all in. And be sure to let the other animals enjoy a bit of the limelight too. Wild dogs, gaur, spotted deer, leopard, wild boar – they should all get some quality time with the tourists.

'And don't forget the birds! Eagles, hornbills, storks, vultures and of course the peacocks. They all add to the overall magic of a jungle safari and it's only after you let them experience the rest of Tigeropolis that you move on to the main attraction: an encounter with their first tiger and an opportunity to take a good photo to show off to friends back home.'

'How long should we give them?' asked Tala.

'I'd say ten or fifteen minutes max,' replied Vinni. 'Always remember: when it comes to tiger spotting, less is more. Tiger watching should be a special time; the real highlight of a game drive.

'But how do you cope with all the attention?' asked Raj, 'doesn't it all get too much? From what you're saying, it must be impossible to go out anywhere without being hassled. People wanting selfies and camera flashes going off in your face all the time, it must be awful. Not a moment's peace.'

'No, it's fine really, you get used to it,' said Vinni, matter-of-factly. 'Most people are quite well-mannered and they don't tend to get too close. Don't know why, but one smile from me, and they seem to back off (he grinned). Also, it seems tourists don't like being out in the hottest part of the day and they stay in their dens (sorry hotels) at night. So for the most part, you're pretty much on your own.

'And, of course, there's one big perk of being the celebrity in any park…'

'What's that?' asked Tala.

'We always get the best spots at the water hole,' said Vinni, clearly enjoying his life in the spotlight. 'Even the elephants stand aside when we arrive. And absolutely everyone wants to have you at their event, so you get invited to everything that's anything and you can take your pick.'

'Tell me about the tourists,' Raj interjected, keen to get back to business.

'Well, we usually get four main types,' explained Vinni. 'First, there are *The Young Couples*. Always in a hurry, never much time anywhere, as they're trying to see the world before they settle down. So with them, it's very much "today it's tigers, tomorrow trekking in Tibet," next week they're off bungee jumping in Bermuda.'

'Next are *The Family Groups*. They're really excited to be here, but the kids do tend to be a bit restless in the jeeps and get easily bored. So the drivers need to be always spotting something new for them to see and discover.

'Then there are *The Retired.* Nice people, probably on a trip of a lifetime. They'll be very interested in everything they see but – and this is very important – they're just as concerned to get a cup of tea and a scone when they get back to the lodge at the end of the day.

'They can also be a bit slow with their cameras. Easily confused. They never have the right glasses to hand... so best to avoid sudden movements as they'll never get you in focus otherwise.

'One thing they all have in common is that they're here for the overall experience, so remember that. They're really not too demanding, all-in-all. The key thing is that they all get at least one nice picture, ideally of me. Yawning conspicuously, giving them a flash of my fangs glinting in the sun, sitting by the roadside, that sort of thing. Even better if the sun's setting... the colours at that time of day are just amazing.'

'What about the fourth type?' asked Raj, finally beginning to appreciate just how much work was involved in keeping the tourists happy.

'Ah, yes,' Vinni went on, 'then there are *The Explorers* or, as I call them the men in wide-brimmed hats. All very dashing, or at least they'd like to be. They really want to get involved. Given half a chance, they want to try out their tracking and hunting skills.

'They're nice guys but I think they probably imagine they're like the tiger hunters of old. They must have read too many *Boy's Own* adventure stories when they were young, *Giggles* and *The Beagle*, that sort of thing…

'In reality, most of them wouldn't say boo to a goose, and they're quite happy to play a sort of hide-and-seek with you. So, if you spot them, duck down out of sight.

Let them guess where you might be as you move stealthily through the bush. To make it work, you need to break the odd twig here and there and make a nice *snap* that they can hear. Give them a clue where you are. And leave some good paw prints. Nothing gets them more excited than fresh scat or a nice clean pug mark in the sand. Occasionally, for fun, I take my pug stamp out with me and leave prints going in two directions at once. That really causes confusion.'

Raj was writing it all down furiously.

Vinni continued, 'Let them catch glimpses of you every 5 minutes or so as you prowl through the '*shadow dappled sal forest*' that they have read about in their guidebooks. And definitely, at least once in the chase, turn and give a deep, loud, growl. But it must be unseen; from deep cover. They want to test their ability to work out exactly where in the forest you must be just from the sounds. Trust me, they'd go wild for such an experience!

'Finally', he said warming to the theme, 'remember they'll love it sooooooooo much if you can get monkeys and other animals to play along, shaking the tree canopy, making alarm calls, that sort of thing.'

'What do you mean, Vinni?' asked Tala, a little unsure why any monkey would want to sound an alarm if Raj or she were about (in Tigeropolis they were on first name terms with each and every one of them).

'It's not that they are *actually* scared of you,' explained Vinni, 'it's really just to add to the general atmosphere of it all. If you can get the monkeys to call out from the high branches, it's just so much more exciting for everyone.

'Ideally you to want to fill the forest full of calls… all the other animals signalling to each other that a tiger's on the prowl. You know, plenty of…

'A–A–A–A–A–A–A–A… Over there! No, over there! A–A–A–A–A–A–A–A… Behind you… A–A–A–A–A–A–A–A!'

'That sort of thing. Total chaos. It's hard work to organize… but if you can get the choreography right, it's so much fun. They'll love it.'

'Makes sense,' said Tala, not totally sure she liked the idea.

'Oh, and there's one exception to these rules,' he went

on, 'Film Crews. They are a different matter entirely. They mean well enough, I suppose, but so much hassle. They stalk you incessantly. They don't just want an hour or two's game drive and a few photos before going back to the lodge for tiffin, they want to take over and you just can't go anywhere, day or night, without their big lenses poking out at you.'

'Oh', said Tala, a little disconcerted at the idea of being constantly spied upon like that.

'I suppose they are under so much pressure from their bosses to get exciting new footage that they don't really think about what it's like for us. It's like being on a reality TV show, but without the prize money at the end.

'But the best of the bunch is not actually a photographer himself, he comes along with them, and seems to stand around just talking. Soft spoken, very knowledgeable. He's not as regular a visitor now, mind you.

'Old fellow… got a name like a cake… Bakewell, Kipling or something like that. Been around TV forever… Battenberg! Yes, that's it. Battenberg. David Battenberg. Been coming here for years.'

'Oh, we know Battenberg,' said Tala excitedly, 'the cubs were watching some of his excellent work on TV recently. Amazing fellow: did a funny one with baby hippos a while back. They splashed him all over while he was busy talking to camera. How I laughed.'

Matti butted in 'he did something with gorillas too and they were just like the tourists we saw today – with their cute wee hands and funny gestures.'

'Yes but he was nearly squashed by them, if I remember rightly,' said Raj.

'That reminds me, I nearly forgot,' said Vinni, 'what are you doing about Health & Safety, Raj?'

'Oh not thought about that Vinni,' admitted Raj, 'do you think we need to worry?'

'Worry?' said Vinni, 'I'll say so. Health & Safety is a very big issue these days. Close you down in a flash if you don't have the right forms and, what's more, any problems and they will cancel your insurance on the spot. End of. Quite dangerous these tourists you know.'

'Oh,' said Raj, looking worried and a bit unsure of what he should say next.

'Key thing,' said Vinni, 'know the risks. You need to work out what might go wrong, how likely it is to happen and what you can do about it – all common sense really, but you need to have it covered and have your paperwork up to date.'

Raj nodded, still concerned it was all getting too complicated.

'I can help you, but probably the main thing is just ensure you don't get too close to the tourists, unless of course they're well caged up,' continued Vinni. 'As long as they're kept inside their jeeps and with their trainers – sorry, guides – then you're probably fine.'

'But don't tourists want to see us hunting?' enquired Tala. 'What are we going to do about that? We're all vegetarians at Tigeropolis these days.'

'Good point!' exclaimed Raj, 'Yes, Vinni, what do we do about that?'

'It's okay. We had exactly that problem here too and got round it by getting in some stunt deer. They're very convincing. We use deer from the west coast: *Deer Devils.*

Great guys. They work on all the big Bollywood films.

'Usually, we chase them for about 400 metres or so, depending on the terrain. A bit of zigging here, a bit of zagging there, and then, on an agreed signal, we pounce. 'Thwack!' he said, hitting his paw down hard on the table to emphasize the point, his sharp claws clacking on the surface.

'Eek,' Matti and Bittu shrieked as they drew back from the table.

'We don't really harm them of course,' Vinni reassured them, 'on cue, the deer fall over and play dead. We then stand tall with one paw on our 'kill' and give out a loud roar to celebrate our victory. Sometimes we use a bit of fake blood too, just to add to the drama.

'Tourists love it and they always seem to get good shots. Great thing is that they don't hang about too long as most are a bit squeamish and, in any event, the guides tell them it's dangerous to be around tigers and their 'kill' as we're supposed to be very protective of our food. So all you need is a couple of minutes or so spent growling away at them and they're off. The sambars can then get up, dust themselves down and we can all get on with our day.

'Get them in to do a hunt once a week or so, but not too regularly. Need to maintain the element of surprise and keep it special. You shouldn't guarantee anything. And, of course, by keeping it a rare event, it also keeps the costs down. We're not due to have them again until next Tuesday. Key person is Anshul, he's the boss, good guy, always delivers and not too expensive either. I'll give you his number.'

'Thanks,' said Raj, visibly impressed at his cousin's planning and business skills.

'So Raj, Tala? What do you think?' asked Vinni.

'I think we're getting there, I really do,' said Raj, 'but perhaps we need a rehearsal first – what do you think cubs? A full rehearsal when we get back?'

'Yes, please!! Please, please, it's so exciting!' they shouted.

Chapter 6 – Debrief

Chapter 7 – Tigers' Return

The early morning mist had finally cleared, with the last wisps rapidly evaporating as the air temperature rose across the meadow. The breeze was fresh, the birds were singing, everything was golden and all was right with the world. Bittu and Matti were padding slowly through the knee-high grass.

Then, in perfect unison, they made their move. Both leapt forward, scattering the little group of sambar that had been grazing peacefully in the sun-dappled meadow. The main group bolted toward the trees, the cubs headed directly for the smallest sambar, who was struggling to keep up with rest. They gave chase as the young sambar dodged under a low hanging branch, shot across the dust track, and raced frantically along the grassy verge.

The cubs were gaining ground quickly: it seemed they were just too powerful for the little sambar. The deer stopped suddenly and quickly doubled back, wrong-footing the cubs. They looked at each other in exasperation. Matti then split off to the right to cover any possible further switch of direction, whilst Bittu kept up in direct pursuit.

In a few moments he was back within striking distance and, fatefully, the sambar glanced round to see how close his pursuers were. Bittu seized his chance, found an extra spurt of energy and leapt forward, sending both of them flying. They rolled together in the dust in a deadly embrace for a moment, then froze. Ten seconds later Bittu got up, put his front paw on the back of the motionless sambar that was now lying face down on the sand, and roared triumphantly:

'ROARRRRR!'

'Cut!' shouted Anshul. 'Great. Well done both of you. Did you get all that Raj?'

'Yes,' replied Raj as he lifted his head from the viewfinder, 'perfect as far as I could see. We can analyse the footage fully when we get home, but I think they all did really well, and Bittu certainly kept his body between the camera and Picca, just as you taught him. And Matti cutting off the escape was a great idea: gave the scene some added sense of scale.'

'Yes, and I thought Picca fell quite beautifully, so balletic,' said Tala.

'Thank you,' said Anshul grinning proudly, 'she learnt it all from her father of course.'

'Yes it's all down to Dad's training,' said Picca as she approached them, dusting herself down.

Picca scribbled a few notes and continued, 'Bittu, you were fractionally late with your leap. I had to anticipate it a bit, which is fine, but remember it's a count of ten *immediately* after we pass the white marker post, following the double back, not ten metres later. If you're late like that in the real thing I'll already be on the ground before you strike. And please... please keep your claws well tucked in – I don't want you scratching me, or breaking a nail when you land.

'Matti you were great, but you need to be a bit more aggressive when you arrive on scene. You need to suggest you might just take the kill from your brother if you don't get your share. More menace. Apart from that, great job.'

'My little perfectionist,' said Anshul admiringly. 'It's going to be great, I just know it.'

'Yes. Well done everyone,' said Tala.

Bittu smiled. Who would have thought it? Two weeks ago he could never have imagined that he would be working with some of Bollywood's finest. Anshul had even been in the great Glint Westwood's chapati westerns of the past. *The God, the Buddha and the Ugli Fruit* was one of his all-time favourites. He played The Deer with No Name: and what a performance! This was certainly much more fun than school.

Raj, imagining himself managing a new tourist empire, announced, 'well, I think this is the final piece of the jigsaw – we're ready. I think we can safely claim our training a success and now we're ready for business.'

'Hurrah!' shouted Bittu and Matti in unison. In just over ten days they'd learnt everything they needed to know about being wild tigers: how to roar, how to stalk, how to pose, how to hunt; all that remained was to get the news out – people needed to know: *The Tigers are back at Tigeropolis!*

Matti had an idea. 'Why don't we post some pictures on *Tigerbook* and *Indigram*, and of course we could cheep it out too?'

'Great idea,' said Raj, 'we can use that nice shot of the cubs we took yesterday by the old fort – the fort is unmistakably Tigeropolis.'

'I think we should also get a shot of you, Raj, perhaps guarding the old temple steps. People will love the idea of a wise old tiger free to roam through a ruin like that,' said Tala.

'Shouldn't we have a copy of someone holding today's newspaper just as they do in the movies when the kidnapper has to prove it's a recent photo and the people are still alive?' asked Matti, 'after all, we are trying to show we are here, and here now.'

'Not necessary,' said Bittu, 'all the photos are time-stamped.'

And so they uploaded the photos and Raj, who was old-fashioned and thought he needed to cater for all sorts, also sent a copy in the post to the Delbai Times and,

just to be doubly sure the news got out, he also placed a small ad in the local paper, the Hindustan Moon for 250 Rupees.

!!Tourists Wanted!!
No prior experience necessary
Visit Tigeropolis – India's Top Tiger Treat

Three days later, and this time with mother's permission, Bittu and Matti were sitting in the shade, next to the open window of the old chowki hut.

Dring... Dring... went the phone. It didn't often ring, so it gave everyone quite a fright when it did. In the office the two guards looked at each other trying to decide who should answer. Neither really liked answering the phone as it was all a bit too modern for their liking. The older guard lent forward to pick up the black, bakelite receiver.

'Forest Officer Mistry speaking. Can I help you?'

A woman's voice said 'hello Mr Mistry, Minister of Forests and Tourism here.'

'It's the Minister!' said Forest Officer Mistry in a panicky voice, placing his hand over the mouthpiece as he sought support from his colleague. He had never spoken to anyone so important before. Few people even seemed to know Tigeropolis existed, let alone phoned them. But a Minister? Well, it was all too much.

'What should I say?' he whispered to his colleague, still cupping the mouthpiece with his hand.

'Mr Mistry? Are you there...? Mr Mistry?' demanded the voice on the other end impatiently. 'Mr Mistry?'

Oh dear, he thought to himself. He had to say something. And fast.

'Here Madam! Yes, here Your Majesty. I mean at your service Madam... I mean, Madam Minister, Sir.' It was the best he could manage in the circumstances.

'Mr Mistry,' said the voice on the other end of the phone, seemingly oblivious to what he had actually said,

'I'm just phoning to say we have all seen the posts, the pictures and the ten thousand re-cheeps. It's a phenomenon! It's wonderful news, wonderful. How did you do it?'

Mr Mistry struggled to think of a reply, not least because he hadn't the faintest idea what the Minister could be taking about - they weren't online and hadn't bought a paper in months, so they knew nothing of what was happening in the outside world.

But he didn't have to worry. The Minister was far too busy talking to actually worry about any response. She continued on, 'to think that on *my* watch, tigers have been sighted once again in Tigeropolis… simply wonderful, fully justifies my far-sighted policy of centralized devolvement and the faith the nation has placed in me and in our *Long Term Plan* these last few months! Yes, full vindication of our policy.'

'Ahhh, yes Minister, indeed yes, quite so, congratulations,' said Mr Mistry still rather bemused at what this could all mean, but feeling he had better agree nonetheless. Before he could add anything, the Minister was back in full flow.

'So well done for all your hard work in making it happen, Mr Mistry. Truly wonderful... and after so much negative news about Tigeropolis recently! Can't think why people even suggested closing such a valuable wildlife refuge. And you can forget any talk of a road: the tigers are just too important... no, a road... that most definitely won't be happening. Not with our *Long Term Plan*. Conservation is the key.

'Now, yes. I was just saying to Sadeep here, by my side... I always knew that fellow... Mistry, that is your name isn't it? That Mr Mistry was an achiever, he'll go far. Granted I've not actually heard of anything you've ever done in the last twenty years I've been in charge, but you're an achiever nonetheless... I'm sure. You're overdue a promotion. I just want to say Tigeropolis is an inspiration to us all. Yes, an inspiration.'

'Thank you Madam Minister... it's a team effort of course,' said Mr Mistry just a little embarrassed and also somewhat conscious that his young colleague was able to hear what was being said.

'I can't wait to personally welcome the first tourist when the park reopens after the monsoon, Mr Mistry...

My office will be in touch about the arrangements… the press… the TV… Yes… perfect… Great photo opportunity… especially with the election looming… Goodbye.' And at that point, there was a click and the line went dead.

Mr Mistry put down the receiver somewhat stunned and surprised. 'Well, well, well. I've no idea what that was about, but it seems HQ are happy… something about tigers out on the road in the monsoon and the press coming here in October.' He got up to make some tea to calm himself down. It had been such an exhausting morning.

Akash knew it had been a risk leaving Mr Mistry to answer the phone. He always got nervous talking to anyone he didn't know personally. However, he also knew that it was not too risky as he'd find out soon enough if it was important. And this clearly was important: it involved a Minister.

In fact he knew Head Office would send a note, in triplicate and just to make doubly sure they would also send a man. Soon, he'd know exactly what to do. In the meantime, he agreed with Mr Mistry that it was certainly time for tea (and hopefully some cake).

Outside Bittu and Matti were listening just below the open window. They turned and high-fived each other. They had done it! Tigeropolis was saved.

They ran off to tell Uncle Raj and their mum what they'd heard, and, as they scampered off back home, they were already starting to think of the fun to come!

THE END

Glossary

78s – An early analogue audio recording fomat. The modulated sound signal was physically inscribed on a spiral grove in the record's surface. The term 78 referred to the Revolutions Per Minute (RPM) required when playing the record to ensure accurate reproduction of the original sound.

Aloo Puri – Spicy potatoes (aloo) with puffed whole bread (puri).

Banyan Tree – The National tree of India. A type of fig tree that seeds on other trees and gradually dominates. It is characterised by a complex pattern of aerial roots that hang down from the branches of a host tree to form a sort of curtain.

Bakelite – An early form of plastic – usually black.

Chai/Masala Chai – Spiced milk tea.

Chowki – A small police/guard post – also derivation of an old fashioned UK slang term for prison – chokey.

Dal – Dried split lentils/peas, can also be made into a thick stew.

Durbar – Grand ceremonial gathering and parade during which lesser princes and nobles paid their respects to a ruler.

Phonograph/Record Player – A mechanical device for listening to recorded music (similar in concept to a wind-up MP3 player).

Gaur – Indian Bison – a large animal similar to a cow.

Howdah – A seat used when riding on top of elephants that can be highly decorated. It can usually accommodate at least 2 people and often has a canopy.

Langurs – Large grey monkeys with black face and ears, found across India.

Mahoot – A person that is in charge of, and looks after, a working elephant.

Pakora – Deep fried snack (may be made of a variety of ingredients).

Parathas – Unleavened flatbread, common in Northern India.

Paneer Masala – Vegetarian dish made from cottage cheese.

Pug Mark – An animal footprint (pug is an Indian word for foot). It is most commonly used to describe tiger tracks.

Rotis – Unleavened flatbread (see also Parathas above).

Rupee – Indian unit of Currency 1 Rupee, (roughly equivalent to 1 UK Pence).

Sal Tree/Forest – The Sal tree is common across North India – huge with dark-green leaves and orange/yellow blossom. Buddhists believe Buddha passed away while lying between two Sal trees that spontaneously burst into blossom.

Sambar Deer – A deer species, common across North India.

Scat – Animal droppings

Shellac – A resin secreted by the female Lac bug in trees in the forests of India. Hard plastic-like material used in the manufacture of old-fashioned 78 rpm records.

Tigeropolis – Probably the best Tiger park in all India and home to its most enterprising tigers. It is located somewhere between Delhi and the Himalayas.

Acknowledgements

I would like to thank some of the very many people who helped or inspired me to write this book.

Thanks go to… Julian Matthews who happily let me invite myself to join part of his three month quest to visit each and every one of India's tiger parks, and who, it seems, can quite literally sleep through a herd of wild elephants stampeding through camp after just one glass of the local brew. Vikramjit Singh Bal deserves a mention for his many patient hours explaining things to me and how could I forget the inspirational Kay & Satyendra Tiwari. Also a mention to Sir Richard and Lady Arabella Stagg for their generous hospitality over many visits – even if I did get kicked out of bed one morning at 5 am with some vague story about needing my bed for a VIP that 'state security' forbade them to name. I'd also like to thank Andrew Cook for his crisp, clear and imaginative design, Grace Anderson for the original title design and early concept drawings and Ross Burridge for his early proof reading and general enthusiasm. Thanks too to the team at Beehive for leading us to Matt Rowe – his illustrations have caught the essence of the characters and have really brought the book to life in a way that I know fully meets with the approval of Bittu, Matti, Tala and Raj. Finally I have to thank Kay who, not only helped edit the final text, but did so much more to actually bring it all together and make it the book that you hold in your hands today.

R.D. Dikstra.

About the Author

R. D. Dikstra was born and brought up in Scotland and has lived in London for most of his life. He became interested in wildlife conservation after spending two weeks whale watching in Alaska. He first visited a tiger park in 2009 and immediately recognized that these were important places that needed to be protected. He stumbled on the Tigeropolis story not long after his first ever tiger sighting.

Look out for other Titles in the Tigeropolis Series -

Book 2

The Grand Opening

Book 3

Caught in the Trap

www.tigeropolis.co.uk